This Book Belongs to

_____

Nutcracker

by E. T. A. Hoffmann

Retold by Fiona Black

Illustrated by

Scott Gustafson

BARNES
& NOBLE
BOOKS
NEW YORK

Nutcracker

Nutcracker

It was Christmas Eve. The Stahlbaum family was gathered around a tall Christmas tree that was beautifully decorated with glowing candles, candied apples, and sugar almonds. The children, Fritz and Marie, were playing with their new presents when a strange little man with long white hair and a black patch over one eye entered the room.

Nutcracker

"Godpapa Drosselmier," the children cried happily as they rushed to him. Despite his odd appearance, their godfather was very kind and clever. He could fix any watch or clock, and he had made them many remarkable toys, too.

"Merry Christmas!" said Godpapa Drosselmier as he handed each child a present. Fritz's gift was a set of tin soldiers, each carrying a handsome sword. Marie's gift was a little wooden man in a bright red uniform.

"Please take good care of this little fellow, Marie," her godfather said solemnly. "He means a great deal to me!"

Marie took the little man in her arms. Despite his elegant uniform and bright paint, he was rather ugly. His head was far too big for his body, and his mouth cut from ear to ear!

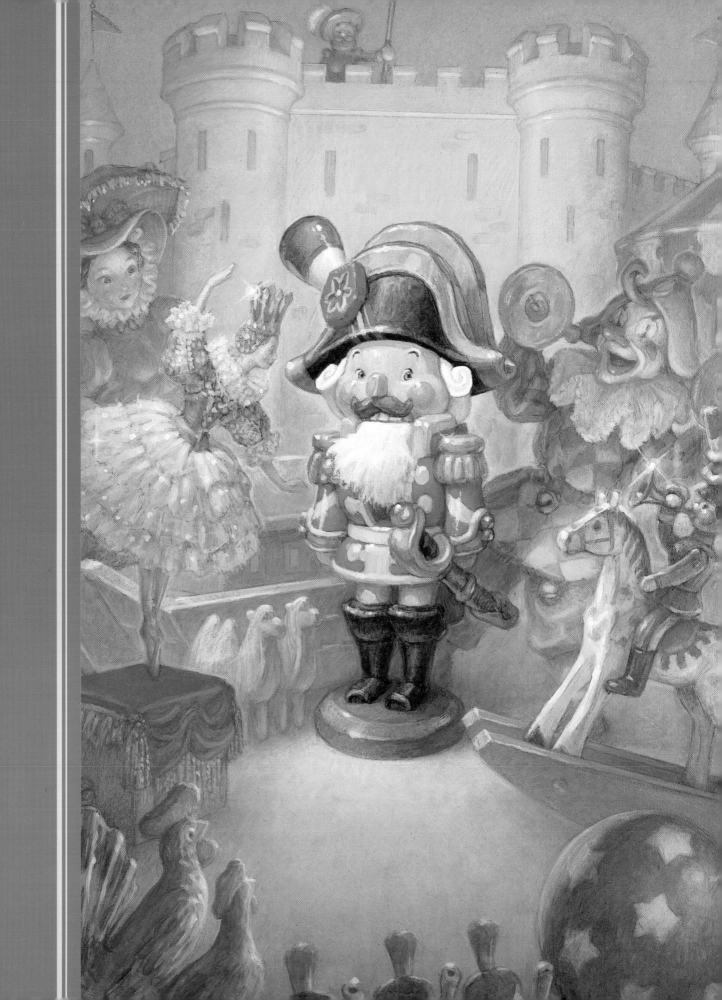

Nutcracker

"Why, it's a nutcracker!" cried her father. Then he showed Marie how to put a nut in the little man's mouth and shut it tight. There was a quick crack, and the nutshell fell to the floor.

Marie hugged the nutcracker. "Thank you, Godpapa," she cried. "He is my favorite present!"

"How can you like such an ugly fellow?" said Fritz scornfully.

"Don't say that," cried Marie. "You'll hurt his feelings!"

"I'm afraid Fritz is right," Godpapa Drosselmier said. "Our poor nutcracker is rather ugly. If you like, I'll tell you the story of how ugliness came into his family."

Nutcracker

"Oh, please do!" begged the children.

"Very well," began their godfather. And this is the tale he told.

Many years ago there lived a king who had a very beautiful daughter. Her name was Princess Pirlipat. She had golden hair and rosy cheeks. Her father adored her and one year he planned a great feast in honor of her birthday.

Now the king was very fond of sausages, and the queen always made them herself. So in honor of the celebration the king asked his wife to make three hundred of her best sausages.

Nutcracker

Just as the queen had finished making them, Dame Mouserink, the queen of mice, came into the kitchen. "Let me taste a bit of sausage!" she squeaked.

"Of course," the queen replied. Then Dame Mouserink, followed by all her greedy relations, pounced on the sausages and ate them all up!

When the king learned what had happened he was furious. He announced that whoever rid the kingdom of mice would win the princess's hand in marriage.

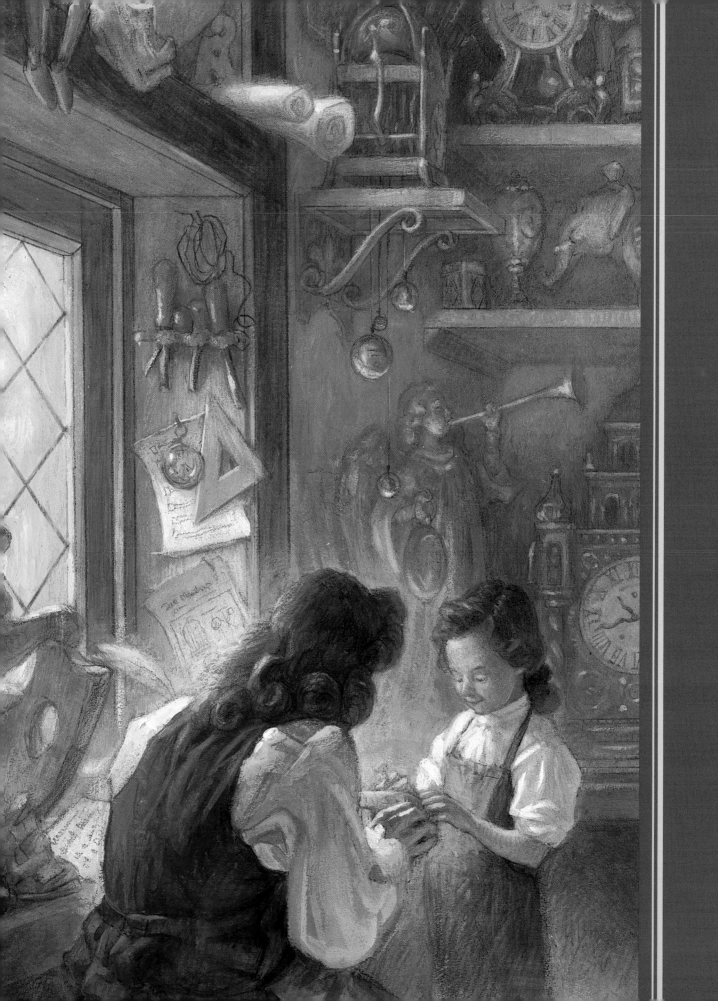

Nutcracker

Now, one of the king's closest advisors was a clever clockmaker. This clockmaker had a nephew. The boy had been orphaned as a baby and raised by the clockmaker. The nephew was a charming, handsome young man and had the remarkable ability of cracking even the hardest nuts with his teeth. Everyone called him, "The Handsome Nutcracker."

The clockmaker decided it would be a fine thing if his nephew married the beautiful Princess Pirlipat. So he began to plan the world's first mousetrap. He baited his traps with sausage. Then he had his nephew set the traps throughout the palace. All of Dame Mouserink's greedy relatives were soon trapped and put to death. But Dame

Nutcracker

Mouserink herself was far too clever to become caught in such a way.

Nevertheless, the king was overjoyed and summoned the clockmaker's nephew. With great fanfare he announced that the boy could one day marry the lovely princess.

Nutcracker

No sooner had he spoken than Dame Mouserink appeared and made this pronouncement:

I, queen of mice, pronounce this curse:

The Handsome Nutcracker shall become
*   hideously ugly.*
And for him I predict the worst:

My son, the mouse with seven crowns,
Will surely bring the Nutcracker down!

The king's soldiers quickly fell on Dame Mouserink and killed her. Then Princess Pirlipat looked at the clockmaker's nephew and shrieked, "Oh, how ugly he is! I will never marry him!" You see, the clockmaker's handsome nephew had changed. He now had a huge misshapen head.

The clockmaker was heartbroken and felt he was to blame for his nephew's misfortune.

Nutcracker

So he visited a famous astrologer to learn how the spell might be broken.

"Do not despair," the astrologer reported after studying the boy's stars. "Your nephew is such a fine young man that he will win a kingdom of his own. But unless he defeats Dame Mouserink's son—the Mouse with Seven Crowns—and wins a lady's heart despite his ugliness, he will never return to his proper form."

Nutcracker

"And so," finished Godpapa Drosselmier, "now you know how the mousetrap was invented and why nutcrackers are so ugly."

"What was the clever clockmaker's name?" asked Fritz.

His Godpapa smiled strangely. "Drosselmier," he replied. "Just like mine."

By now it had grown late, and Mrs. Stahlbaum told the children it was time to put their new toys away and go to bed.

Fritz quickly put his soldiers in the toy cabinet in the corner of the room and climbed the stairs to his bedroom. But Marie begged to stay up a little while longer. "I want to put my nutcracker to bed properly," she explained.

Nutcracker

After everyone else had gone to bed, the sitting room seemed dark and mysterious. Marie stared into the nutcracker's painted blue eyes. They had such a sad expression that she wondered if her Godpapa's story could be true. "Don't worry, dear nutcracker," she whispered. "I will help you if I can!"

Then the room filled with rustling and rattling noises. Startled, Marie looked around. The clock, which had started to strike the hour, whirred to a stop. Then Marie heard a voice say:

Clocks, listen and stop your ticking.
Now the mouse king is awakening.
In the light of the full moon
Comes the hour of the nutcracker's doom!

Nutcracker

At that, hundreds of mice began squeezing through all the cracks in the wall and floor.

They organized themselves into troops and marched in place. Then the floor cracked open and from the crack rose a horrible creature—a mouse with seven heads. The seven heads grew from one huge body, and each was topped by a shining crown. The seven heads called the mouse army to order, and they began marching toward the toy cabinet!

Nutcracker

Marie was terrified, but then she heard
another voice cry:

Awake! For the hour has come
When we must fight for our kingdom.
Come, toys, and follow me,
The nutcracker calls to thee!

Nutcracker

Then the nutcracker came marching out of the cabinet with his sword drawn. Marie's dolls and Fritz's tin soldiers leaped down from their shelves in the cabinet and followed him.  They were joined by the teddy bears, the puppets, and the stuffed cotton clown.

With the nutcracker leading, the toys bravely advanced toward the mouse king's army. Fritz's tin soldiers loaded their cannons with lemon drops and hazelnuts and fired at the mice. But little by little the mice gained the

Nutcracker

advantage. They bit the puppets and the stuffed cotton clown and knocked over Fritz's tin soldiers. They soon surrounded the nutcracker.

"Prepare to meet your doom!" squealed the mouse king's seven heads as he scurried toward the nutcracker.

Marie's heart was beating so fast she thought she would faint. But she knew she had to do something to save her friend. So she took off her shoe and threw it at the mouse king.

Then everything around her seemed to grow dark and she fell to the floor.

Nutcracker

When Marie opened her eyes, all traces of the battle had vanished. The nutcracker stood beside her holding his sword in one hand and the mouse king's seven crowns in the other.

"Dear Miss Stahlbaum," he said, "thanks to your courage I was saved from certain death. Please come with me. I have marvelous things to show you!" Then he helped Marie to her feet and opened the door of the toy cabinet.

To her amazement Marie found that she was small enough to step inside the toy cabinet. A bright light washed over her. Then she found herself in a meadow that glittered with a rainbow of colors. "This is Candy Meadow," the nutcracker said. "We are in my kingdom, which is called Toyland."

Nutcracker

He led Marie through a gate made of raisins and almonds and down a road of brightly colored hard candies. Soon they were in a gingerbread town where gingerbread men and women waved at them as they passed.

They came to another town. This one was made of spun sugar and dainty china and glass people sang to them.

"Now we must cross Lake Rosa to the capital of Toyland," the nutcracker said.

Nutcracker

As he spoke, Marie saw a beautiful rose-colored lake and on it there was a little gold boat pulled by dolphins. She and the nutcracker stepped into the boat and were soon pulled across the lake. Ahead, Marie could see a beautiful city made of sugar plums and candied fruits. But most wonderful of all was a lofty castle with tall rose-colored spires.

"This is my home, Marzipan Castle," said the nutcracker.

Elegantly dressed little dolls greeted them, "Hail to the King of Toyland!" Up until then Marie had been too dazzled by everything she

Nutcracker

saw to say a word. But now she turned to the nutcracker and cried, "Then Godpapa's story is true, and you are his nephew!"

"Yes," replied the nutcracker. "With your help, I have defeated the mouse king and won

Nutcracker

back my kingdom, and yet . . ." He sighed so sorrowfully that Marie was sure he must be thinking of the lovely Princess Pirlipat, who had refused his hand.

"I don't understand why the princess was so mean," Marie said, feeling very sorry for the nutcracker. "I would have remained your friend and companion no matter what you looked like. I would not have minded one bit if you were in the shape of a nutcracker!"

Nutcracker

As soon as Marie had spoken, a strange thing happened. The castle around her wavered and then disappeared, and Marie felt as if she were falling and falling.

When she landed she was lying in her own bed, and her mother was standing over her. "Wake up, Sleepy Head," Mother said. "It is Christmas morning."

"Oh, Mother," Marie said. "So much has happened!" And she told her mother about the nutcracker and the mouse king and her visit to Toyland.

"You have had a long, beautiful dream," her mother said. "But now you must get up. We have visitors. Godpapa Drosselmier is here with his nephew."

Marie quickly dressed and ran downstairs. In the sitting room beside the toy cabinet

Nutcracker

stood her godpapa. Beside him was a handsome young man just her age. His eyes were as blue and kind as those of her own dear nutcracker. Marie knew that she had not been dreaming after all.

Godpapa Drosselmier left the two children alone. Then his nephew knelt before Marie. "Dear Marie Stahlbaum," he said, "by pledging to be my friend despite my ugliness, you

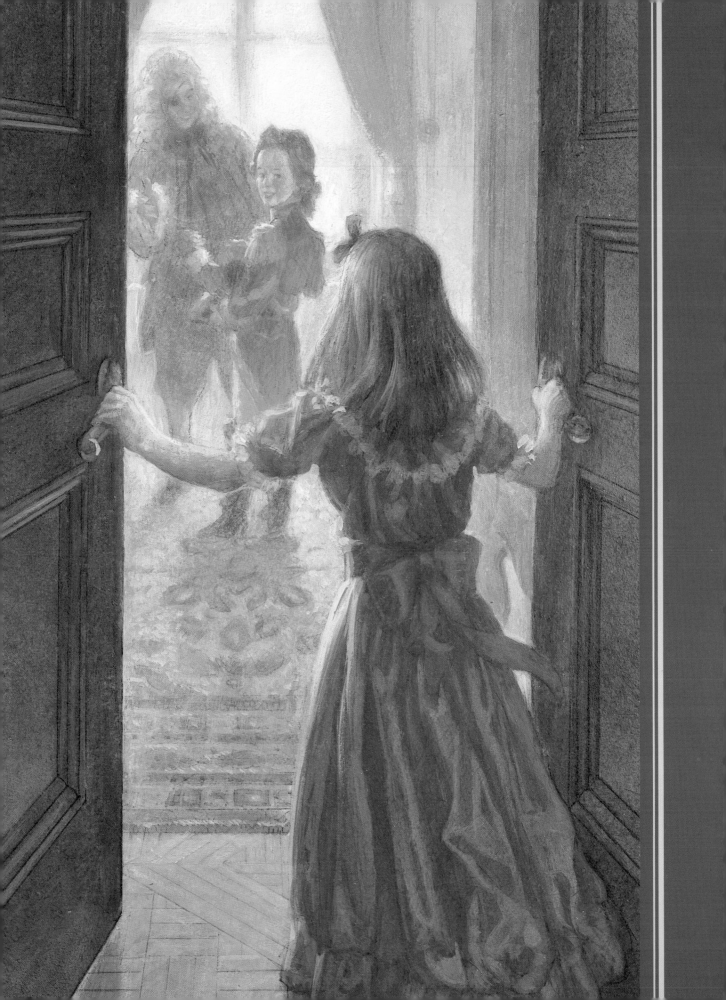

have broken Dame Mouserink's curse. Now I beg you to be my friend always and to rule with me over my kingdom."

Marie smiled and said, "Oh, yes!" And when she was grown up, she married young Drosselmier. Then they went to the Marzipan Castle, and today they still rule over the magical Kingdom of Toyland.